WHAT PETE ATE

from

A - Z

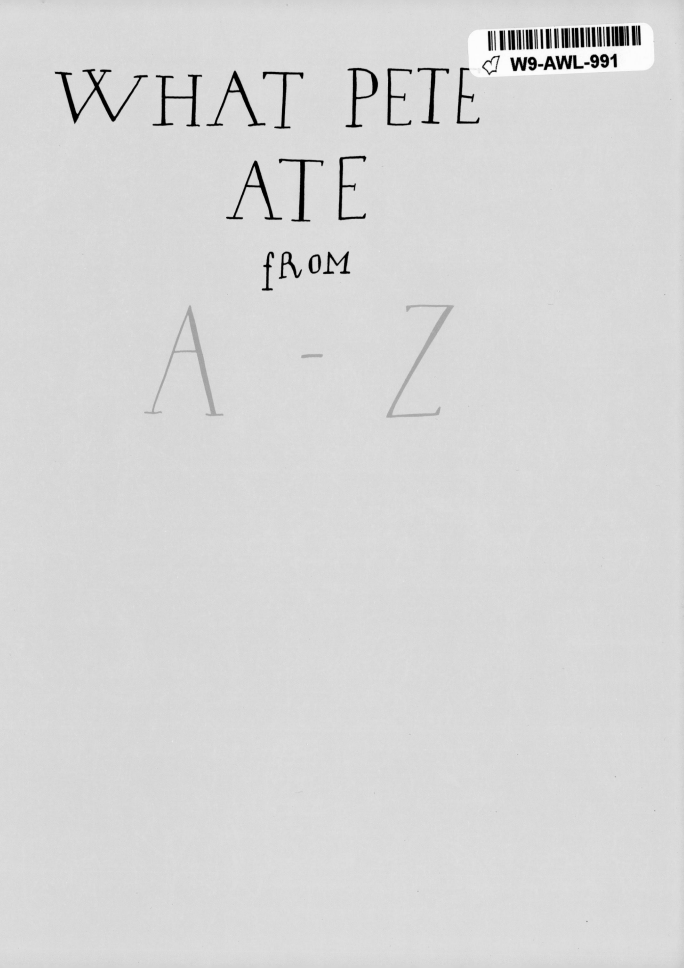

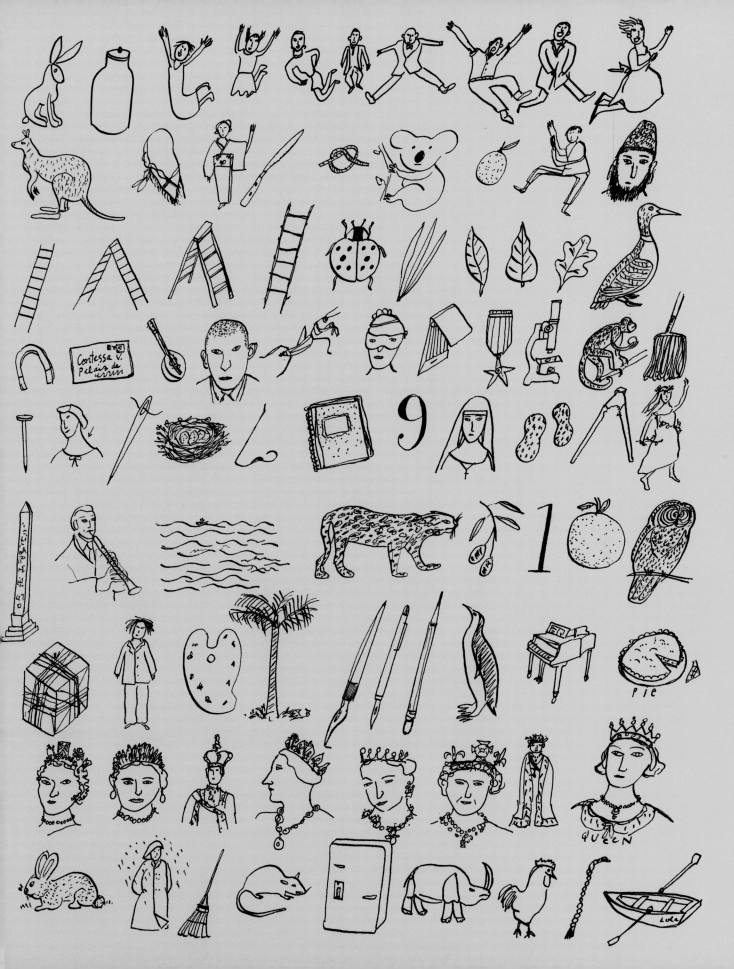

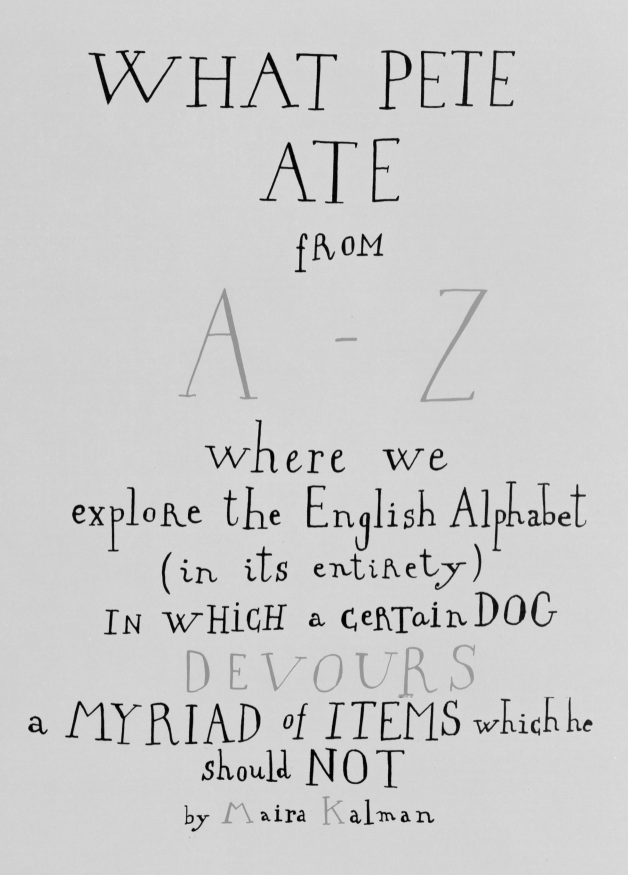

WHAT PETE ATE

FROM

A - Z

where we explore the English Alphabet (in its entirety) IN WHICH a CERTAIN DOG DEVOURS a MYRIAD of ITEMS which he should NOT

by Maira Kalman

PUFFIN BOOKS

My name is Poppy Wise.

This is my little brother MOOKIE

and this is my dog PETE.

A good dog.
A VERY GOOD DOG.
But sometimes he is not
so good. He eats what he
should NOT. WHAT?
I will start with A.

a   A   a

apple

He ate cousin Rocky's accordion.

All of it.

b B b

He ate a bouncing ball that belonged to uncle Bennie's dog Buster.

BOB'S BALL

FEZ F

(Buster is no bargain. He barks all the time, but still...)

Bennie lived in a beautiful room that had a Bed, a Book, a Box, and a Bottle of water.

(And some other things that don't begin with B.)

He did NOT eat the cake from Olga, or the creamy cupcake. NO!

He ate my CAMERA!!
I LOVE to take pictures.
Look.

Baby Mookie eating noodles.

My best friend Doreen Parsley, the great dancer.

d   D   d

He ripped the
head off my
dear doll Dinky.

Dreadful dog.

e E e

While Doreen and I
were making egg salad sandwiches
for the Egghead Club, Pete ran off with
EVERYTHING.

Egg slicer

Eggbeater

Egg Sandwich

Common Cuckoo egg

Emu egg

Chinese Bulbul egg

Egads! Doesn't Pete know the difference between **edible** and inedible?

Edible	Inedible
apple	accordion
bread	ball
cake	camera
cupcake	doll
egg sandwich	eggbeater
honey	fez
ice pop	glue stick
jelly beans	homework
veal roast	money

f   F   f

He ate a FEZ.

LUX

FEZ is also a city in a
country called
MOROCCO
in a continent
called
AFRICA.

(Not everyone
in Fez
wears a
fez.)

G

While the Twinkle Twins were gluing together Mookie's Halloween costume, Pete GOBBLED the glue stick with Gusto.

GOOFY GLUEY DOG.

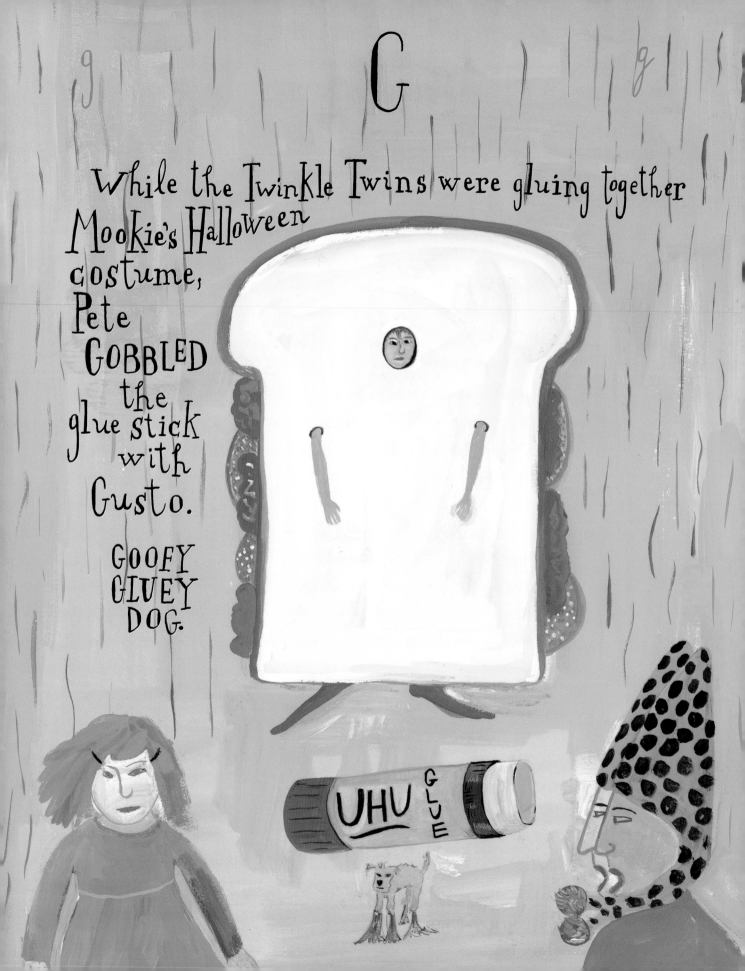

h   H   h

HAT

HIPS

BIG HAIR-DO

1 + 1 =

He ate half ($\frac{1}{2}$) of my homework. But did Mrs. Hoogenschmidt believe me? HA! (HARDLY.) HORRIBLE dog.

i   I   i

When I turned my back for an itsy
iota of time, he ate my beautiful pink
ice pop.

j   J   J

In a
jiffy
he ate 25
jelly beans

and he jumped for joy.

K

k   k

He ate MooKie's magic KEY.

The Key
opened
Mookie's secret box.
What's inside
is a SECRET, but
I will tell only You.
(It is his KAZOO.)

At the Lucky Dog Show, he ate
all the leashes which let loose all

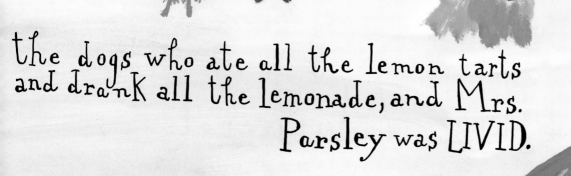

the dogs who ate all the lemon tarts and drank all the lemonade, and Mrs. Parsley was LIVID.

I don't want to make a
mountain out of a molehill,

Real (NO KIDDING) Money

But, he ate Bennie's money.

Holy Mackerel !

Buster says, "Nuts to Pete."

Now Bennie has no money (NONE) to buy Buster a new ball which, you will remember, Pete ate many letters ago.

n N n

H, once in a while we go into the woods and Pete is Perfect. Then I am of the opinion that this dog is O.K.

Oops,

we are up to P p p

He ate Mrs. Parsley's pink pocketbook and she said, "Take that Pete back to the Pet Shop and get yourself a polite pooch."

Pooh on Mrs. Parsley.

q   Q   q

Quick Question.
Would you love a dog who ate your
lucky quarter, the Q from your
alphabet collection, your porcupine quill?
Even if for the quadrillionth time
you said, "Quit It.
Don't EAT that,"
and he Did, would
you still love that
dog?

Quite a lot.

R r r

One Rainy day,
he ate a rubber glove
and the rubber band
necklace
Mrs. Parsley
wore to a
meeting of the
Rubber Band Society.

Roberta Rothschild
is the President of the
Rubber Band Society.

Now Pete Bounces
around the Room.

S

He ate Mookie's
stinky sneaker for
breakfast.
Doreen Parsley's
sandal for lunch.

Rocky's pointy
shoe from Japan
for dinner.

And a soft suede
slipper for a
midnight snack.

S

t   T   t

The Twinkle Twins have a dog named Twinky.
Twinky may look insane, but she
does not eat their things.

u U u

You can understand that I would
be Unhappy to say this, but Pete
ate cousin Rocky's underpants.

Uggh!

While Mookie was playing the violin (very badly thank you very much) Pete ran off with the veal roast. VERY angry and hungry family.

W   W

What can I say?

In his wallet,
Rocky keeps a
list of all the
times he was
insulted his
whole life.

It used to look
like this.

Who
What
When
Where
Why

(list on scroll, partially legible)
POPPY was
late by 5 minutes
BENNIE was
LATE
someone did
not say
GOOD MORNING
POPPY borrowed
my book and
did not return
Doreen did not
say thank you
when I gave
her a
lollipop
George did
not say thank
you when I
did not sit
Never did
a nice thing
Did not say
you're welcome
...
There were
NO FISH

Now it looks
like this.

WOW.

(Personally, I am happy Pete did it.)

x X x

X-TRA CHEEZY
CHEEZ
Doodles

When Pete eats
X-tra CRUNCHY X-tra Cheezy
CHEEZ DOODLES,
he turns
BRIGHT
ORANGE.

y Y Y y

YiKes!

He ate

Mookie's
yo-yo,

my
yo-yo,

DoReen's
yo-yo

Now there will
be NO Yo-Yo contest.

and the
yo-yos of
the Twinkle
Twins.

Oy-oy
oy-oy
oy-oy
oy-oy
OY.

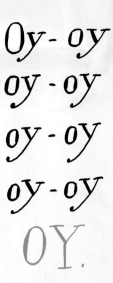

This is what he will <u>not</u> eat.

ZUG ZUG DOG GRUB
(ZIP, ZILCH, ZERO.)

CAN YOU BLAME HIM?

ZOOKS!

WHATTADOG!!

PUFFIN BOOKS, A DIVISION OF PENGUIN YOUNG READERS GROUP. 345 HUDSON STREET, NEW YORK, NY 10014. FIRST PUBLISHED IN THE UNITED STATES OF AMERICA BY G. P. PUTNAM'S SONS, A DIVISION OF PENGUIN PUTNAM BOOKS FOR YOUNG READERS, 2001. PUBLISHED BY PUFFIN BOOKS, A DIVISION OF PENGUIN YOUNG READERS GROUP, 2003. PUBLISHED SIMULTANEOUSLY IN CANADA. PRINTED IN THE UNITED STATES OF AMERICA. DESIGN: JOLLY M&CO. PRODUCTION: MEAGHAN KOMBOL. THE ART WAS DONE IN GOUACHE. THE LIBRARY OF CONGRESS HAS CATALOGED THE G. P. PUTNAM'S SONS EDITION AS FOLLOWS: KALMAN, MAIRA. WHAT PETE ATE FROM A-Z / BY MAIRA KALMAN. P. CM. SUMMARY: IN THIS ALPHABET BOOK, A CHILD RELATES SOME OF THE UNUSUAL THINGS EATEN BY PETE THE DOG, INCLUDING AN ACCORDION, A LUCKY QUARTER, AND UNCLE NORMAN'S UNDERPANTS. [1. DOGS—FICTION. 2. ALPHABET.] I. TITLE. PZ7.K125 WH 2001 [E]—DC21 2001019056 ISBN 0-399-23362-8

2019

PUFFIN BOOKS ISBN 978-0-14-250159-7

THIS BOOK IS FOR MY VERY BELOVED FAMILY (YOU KNOW WHO + WHERE YOU ARE) AND THE EXCELLENT DEAR BEAST HIMSELF. . . .

Yes

YOGU

yoo
hoo

ZOO